Contents

Some words are shown in bold, **like this**. You can find out what they mean by looking in the glossary.

Where Is Pakistan?

To learn more about Pakistan, we meet three children who live there. Pakistan is a country in Asia. It is near India and China.

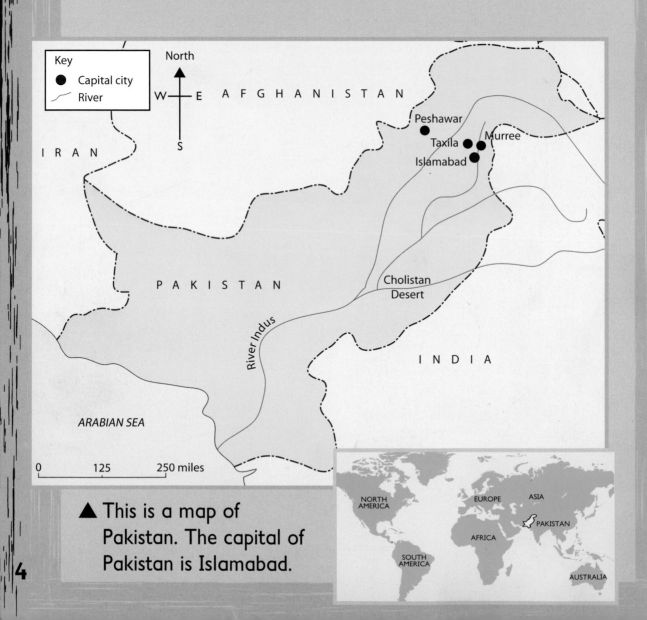

Key
● Capital city
⌇ River

North
W E
S

AFGHANISTAN

IRAN

Peshawar
Taxila   Murree
Islamabad

PAKISTAN

Cholistan
Desert

River Indus

INDIA

ARABIAN SEA

0   125   250 miles

NORTH
AMERICA
EUROPE
ASIA
PAKISTAN
AFRICA
SOUTH
AMERICA
AUSTRALIA

▲ This is a map of Pakistan. The capital of Pakistan is Islamabad.

The weather in Pakistan is mostly hot, but it can be cold in the north. Sometimes there are **earthquakes** in Pakistan. At certain times of the year there are also **monsoons**.

▼ There are busy towns in Pakistan.

▼ Most people in Pakistan live in the countryside.

Meet Kynat

Kynat is eight years old. She lives in Islamabad, the capital city of Pakistan. Kynat lives with her mother, father, and older sister.

Kynat's father

Kynat's mother

Kynat

Kynat's sister

Kynat's mother makes ▶
chapattis for the family.

In the evening, the family eats
a meal together. Kynat's
mother cooks the food. The
family likes to eat rice,
chapattis, and **curry**.

Kynat's School

Kynat goes to school six days a week. She studies math, English, **Urdu**, and art. Kynat likes English, but she does not like math.

▲ There are 50 children in Kynat's class.

Kynat's class practices **cricket** and hockey in the school yard. At playtime, Kynat plays clapping and jumping games with her friends.

◀ Kynat and her sister play jumping games at home, too.

Having Fun

When Kynat is not at school, she likes flying her kite. The roof of Kynat's house is flat. Kynat and her sister can play on the roof. Kynat flies her kite there.

◀ Kynat has **henna** painted on her hands.

Kynat wears a long shirt and loose pants. This is called a *shalwar kameez*. For **festivals**, such as **Eid**, she wears a special *shalwar kameez*.

11

Festivals

There are many **festivals** in Pakistan. People and animals wear special clothes at festival time. They eat food sold at stalls on the street. Sometimes they dance, too.

kite

Every year there is a kite festival in Pakistan. On kite day, lots of people fly their kites. There are hundreds of kites in the sky!

Meet Omar

Omar is seven years old. He comes from the city of Peshawar. Omar lives with his mother, father, younger brother, grandparents, three uncles, and two aunts.

▼ Omar has a large family.

Omar's father

Omar's grandparents

Omar's mother

Omar's brother

Omar

Omar's father makes new clothes for people. He is a **tailor**. His mother works at home. Omar would like to be a doctor when he grows up.

Omar's father is very busy ▶ making new clothes before the **festival** of **Eid**.

At Home

Omar likes to help his mother. He take care of his younger brother, Mosseen, while his mother does her work. He likes playing games with Mosseen.

Omar's favorite food is black-eyed beans and naan bread. His family buys food at the fair when it comes to town. Omar likes to drink the fresh fruit juice that is made at the fair.

Omar's Day

Omar goes to school in the mornings. He has to wear a school uniform. In the afternoon, Omar goes to a class to study the **Qur'an** for an hour.

Omar and his best friend, ▶ Muzammin, are learning to read the Qur'an.

Omar likes taking care of his pet birds. He is also learning to play **cricket**. Sometimes he watches cartoons with his brother.

◀ Omar keeps his pet birds on the roof of his house.

Traveling in Pakistan

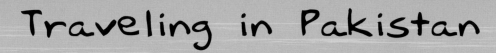

In the towns, people travel in cars. They also travel in large buses. It is cheap to travel in **rickshaws** and in horse-drawn cars.

The buses in Pakistan ▶ can be very colorful.

In the country, there are not many buses or cars so people have to walk. People often walk a long way. Sometimes they carry things on their head as they walk. They also ride on camels.

This girl finds it easier to ▶ hold the heavy pot on her head than in her arms.

Meet Shazia

Shazia is eight years old. She lives in a small village called Cholistan. Shazia lives with her mother, father, brothers, sister, uncle, and aunt.

Shazia's mother

Shazia's aunt

Shazia's sister

Shazia's father

Shazia

Shazia's brothers

Shazia's uncle

Cholistan is in ▶ the **desert**.

Shazia's parents are farmers. ▶
They own a small shop, too.

Shazia's house is made of mud, wood, and straw. They have no water or electricity in the house. There is lots of land around the house where Shazia can play.

23

Life in Cholistan

Shazia and her family look forward to two special **festivals**. One is **Eid** and the other is a spring festival. When there is a festival, Shazia wears a new *shalwar kameez*.

▼ Shazia is learning to sew, so she can make her own *shalwar kameez*.

Cholistan is the hottest, driest part of Pakistan. In the summer there is very little water. Shazia's family has to get water from a deep well.

▲ Shazia's family has a camel. Camels can store water, which helps them live in very hot places.

School and Work

Shazia's school only has one class. Shazia and her brothers and sister are all taught together. They have their lessons outside. Lessons are taught in **Urdu**.

Shazia walks to ▶ school with her father and brother.

After school, Shazia sometimes helps in her parents' shop. She also feeds the farm animals, and helps her mother with the cooking.

▲ The goats are Shazia's favorite animals.

Places to Visit

About 2,000 years ago, many people traveled across Pakistan buying and selling silk. The road they traveled on became famous. It was called the Silk Road. The city of Taxila was on the Silk Road.

▼ Today, people visit the old buildings at Taxila.

◀ Silk and sewing are still important in Pakistan.

cable car

► There is a good view of Murree from the cable car.

Murree is a city in the hills. In the summer, people visit it because it is not as hot as other parts of Pakistan. They travel up the hill by **cable car**.

Pakistani Fact File

Flag   **Capital city**   **Money**

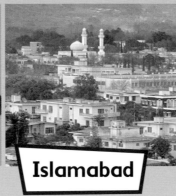

Islamabad

Rupee

Religion
• Around 97 percent of people in Pakistan are Muslims.

Language
• **Urdu** is the official language of Pakistan, but people also speak Punjabi, Sindhi, Siraiki, Pashtu, and English.

Try speaking Urdu!
Subah bakhair .... Good morning.
Kaysay ho? .... How are you?
Bohatt shukria .... Thanks a lot.

Glossary

cable car car that moves along an overhead cable to take people up and down mountains

chapatti thin, flat bread

cricket team sport played with a ball and a flat bat

curry spicy stew of meat, fish, or vegetables

desert very hot, dry area that has almost no rain and very few plants

earthquake sudden movement of the ground caused by rocks under the earth

Eid Eid means "celebration" and is a very important time for Muslims. Eid is at the end of Ramadan, the month of fasting.

festival big celebration for a town or country

henna reddish dye that comes from the leaves of the henna plant

monsoon season of heavy rain

Qur'an Muslim holy book

rickshaw two-wheeled cart with a hood, pulled by one or two people

tailor someone who makes clothes

Urdu official language of Pakistan

More Books to Read

Black, Carolyn. *Pakistan the Culture.* New York: Crabtree Publishing Company, 2002.

Britton, Tamara. *Pakistan.* New York: Checkerboard Books, 2002.

Deady, Kathleen. *Pakisan.* Mankato, Minn.: Bridgestone Books, 2001.

Index